THE HEAVENLY FOX

RICHARD PARKS

PS PUBLISHING EDITION FEBRUARY, 2011

NEW PRINT EDITION OCTOBER, 2020

Table of Contents

Preface

A fox who reaches the age of fifty gains the ability to transform into a human woman. A fox who reaches the age of one hundred can transform into either a beautiful young girl or a handsome gentleman at will and achieves the perception to know everything that is happening around them to a distance of over four hundred leagues. A fox who reaches the age of one thousand years, however, becomes a Heavenly Fox, an Immortal of great power, able to commune with the gods themselves. —Kuo P'u

This text as recorded by the human scholar Kuo P'u in his Hsuan-Chang-Chi describes a fox's true path to immortality, which this worthless book before you will complete and clarify. It will not, however, reveal immortality's great secret, for this cannot be contained, save by those who discover it on their own."

— From the Den and Burrow Guide to Immortality

Part 1: To Live Forever

The main problem with achieving immortality, Springshadow reminded herself, is that you had to live long enough.

That is to say, the preparations for immortality required one thousand years, and one thousand years was not eternity. One thousand years merely seemed like eternity. Especially to Springshadow, who had already counted her nine-hundredth and ninety-ninth birthday almost a year before and felt every one of those birthdays now, though she told the young scholar Zou Xiaofan that she had just turned eighteen. She looked eighteen, and so he believed her. But then, Xiaofan always believed her. Springshadow found that a useful trait in a lover.

"I cannot imagine what my life would have been like without you," he said from his sickbed.

Springshadow understood the irony, but didn't bother to appreciate it. She just smiled and took his hand for a moment after she set the lacquered tray down on the table beside his bed. "Drink your tea. You need to regain your strength."

The rooms Xiaofan rented in the provincial capital were small, merely a bedroom adjoining the slightly larger space he referred to as his "studio". Over the years Springshadow had seen many more rooms that fit the designation better. Even so, like the thousand year fragment of eternity, the differences were more degree than kind. Here on the table was a lump of uncarved jade, there the skull of a badger. Xiaofan's books were arranged on shelves on the far wall, various scrolls and documents in cubbyholes in a small chest near the floor.

When Springshadow took the empty tray away, she noticed something new on the table, a small parchment containing part of a poem, a stiffening, black-tipped brush, and an inkstone in bad need of a cleaning. Springshadow leaned close and read the fragment of poetry. It was about her. The poem, incomplete though it might be, was in Springshadow's opinion a rather lovely piece of verse.

In their short time together, Springshadow had grown fond of Xiaofan in her fashion, but even that miniscule bit of concern was beside the point. The goal — the goal was all that mattered. Three more days were all she needed. No more. No less. In three more days she'd have drawn enough of Xiaofan's living yang energy to brew the elixir that she needed to survive until her next birthday. The most important birthday: her one-thousandth birthday.

"Springshadow?"

"Yes, my love?" she answered immediately. "Do you need something?"

"You," he said. "I need you."

Springshadow closed her eyes, and for a moment her hands balled into fists.

Three days, Xiaofan. If I can wait, so can you, but of course she did not say that. She unballed her fists and composed herself. She kept her voice melodious. "You're not strong enough," she said.

That was a mistake. Springshadow knew it the moment she said it. She should have dropped hints about being "indisposed". She should have changed the subject. But no, she had told the truth. Springshadow steeled herself to deal with

1

the consequences.

"Is there another?"

"What rubbish! Do you think so little of me?" she countered.

"You're young and beautiful. I know you have many admirers."

Springshadow sighed, put down the tray, and returned to the bedroom. Xiaofan had managed to prop himself up against the frame of the bed. Springshadow smiled down on him. "Of course I have many admirers. Yet where am I now? I am here to attend to you in your illness, that's where."

"Because you love me?" he asked.

"I certainly don't love your money," Springshadow said coyly.

That part was true enough. Xiaofan was of good family, but he was not wealthy. He had prospects, of course. He had done well in the regional examinations, and there was reason to think that, once his health had improved, he would perform at least as well in the Imperial Examinations that would determine his status in the bureaucracy that ran the nation. Once he had achieved the rank of Second Level Scholar, he was guaranteed a decent government post, and that was just the beginning. He was an extremely gifted young man. Springshadow knew this to be true, as did Xiaofan. He was also in love with a spirit fox. That was the part that she, alone of the two of them, knew for truth.

"My father is dead. I am now the head of my house, and it is past time for me to take a wife. I want you, Springshadow."

"Lie down now," Springshadow said sternly. "You must save your strength."

"I am not joking." Xiaofan reached into a small chest on a table by his bedside and pulled out a necklace of cylindrical jade beads. He sat up then, so suddenly that Springshadow, surprised, had no time to react. He put the necklace around her neck. "When I am stronger we will have a proper ceremony, but from this day forward I am your husband."

For a moment Springshadow did not know what to do. She considered returning the necklace, but the last thing she wanted just then was a fight with Xiaofan. She knew how weak he was then and why, even if he refused to admit that weakness. "If it pleases you," she said finally. "Now lie down."

His hand was on her arm as she lowered him down on the pillow, surprisingly strong despite his condition. When his head touched the pillow again he did not let go.

"Xiaofan...husband, let me go."

"No," he said. "I cannot. You say you love me. Show me."

Just for a moment, Springshadow considered doing exactly that. All she had to do was drop the necklace on the floor, walk out the door right then, and never see Xiaofan again. He would recover. All would be well with him. In time he would find another, and so would Springshadow.

Yet time was the entire problem. Brewing the Golden Elixir was a delicate matter, and the preparations were arduous with each lover. Perhaps she would have time to start again. Or perhaps the nine hundred and ninety-nine years she had waited would be for nothing. She could take that chance, if she felt strong enough. If her very small bit of affection for Xiaofan outweighed her fear.

She was very afraid.

Springshadow kissed Xiaofan, and then she gave him what he desired. She was as gentle as she dared to be, even though she knew it would make no difference. Xiaofan was weak and far too eager to prove that he was not weak, and just for a few moments, he made her forget his true condition. That time was very short. When it was all done, she adjusted her robes and then held up a glowing, golden ball of light in her two small hands. Xiaofan stared at the ceiling.

"Goodbye, Beloved Husband," she said, but of course he made no answer. Springshadow sighed and found her way out, silent and stealthy as only a fox could be. No one saw her leave. Especially not Xiaofan. Springshadow was certain that the body would not be discovered for days.

She barely made it back to her den in a cave high in the mountains of Shandong. A sudden weakness had come over her. She knew then, if she had waited one more day, she would have been too late. That knowledge wasn't comfort, exactly, since she was a fox and hardly in need of comfort over the death of a human, even one she had some affection for, but she did take the knowledge as justification. She had wanted to give Xiaofan three days to recover, but now she realized her foolishness; she did not have those days to give. It was an odd turn of events, but she knew that Xiaofan's impatience had saved her. Yet, as matters stood, it would still take every bit of her remaining strength and time to complete her task.

Springshadow took the ball of yang male energy that was all that remained of Xiaofan, and she coaxed it into a small cauldron simmering over a fire in her hearth. She chanted the proper spells and stirred in the prescribed manner. Then, when all was ready, she worked the final magics that all foxes knew and converted the yang essence into the Golden Elixir, which she drank while it was still hot. She finally sat down on a stool beside the fire, letting her weariness get the better of her for a little while. The weakness was long gone, and after she had rested a bit, the weariness wasn't quite so heavy. She felt strong.

There was a roll of thunder outside the entrance to her cave, though the day was bright and sunny. Another moment and a shadow fell over the entrance.

"So you did it. I had to come see for myself. And don't bother to get up."

In a roil of clouds and vapor, the Taoist Immortal known as Wildeye strolled into Springshadow's cave. He seemed like an ordinary man, slightly graying hair and beard, middling height. All that set him apart — other than the drama of his entrance — was a faint glow about him that seemed to flicker in ragged ways that had nothing to do with the clouds or wind.

She frowned. "I won't bother, but how did you know about the Elixir? It only happened a few minutes ago."

"I would guess that your sense of time progression would be affected by your impending immortality. But I'm more of the opinion that you're simply preoccupied. Zou Xiaofan's body was discovered three days ago."

"Oh," she said, and that was all.

"Oh? Surely you're not surprised. About the body, I mean, not the matter of your losing track of time."

"He didn't give me a choice," said Springshadow.

3

Wildeye frowned. "You sound defensive. Meaning you made a choice not entirely pleasant to you?"

She shrugged. "If you came to chide me, Wildeye, please yourself. Xiaofan was the last human I used for my own purposes, but he was hardly the first. It was only through my own forbearance that I managed to take what I needed without killing anyone before now. I am sorry for Xiaofan. It would have been pleasant to complete my mission without taking any life at all, but I did what I had to do, and there's the end of it. I've had the final draught of the Golden Elixir that I will require. That's all that matters."

He sat down on a low stool without waiting for an invitation. "Why pleasant?" he asked.

Springshadow blinked. "What do you mean? As a former human, I would think you'd applaud my mercy."

He shrugged. "As a former human? Certainly. But you're not human, former or otherwise. You're a fox Springshadow, and I've known other foxes on the same path you're on. There's not a one of them who left her victim alive at the end, save by accident. Why do you care?"

"I don't. I just thought it would be more...elegant, this way."

"Of course."

"It's not as if their deaths served my purpose as such. It was their living essence I required, not their lives."

"True, though a man drained of his yang essence is scarcely worthy of the name."

"That's not my concern. Besides, too many dead bodies attract attention, which I obviously did not need or want."

"No argument," replied Wildeye, looking disgustingly cheerful.

She scowled at him. "Well, it sounds like an argument."

"I'll just note that your answer keeps changing. Which means you're still thinking about it. Which means you're not sure yourself why you tried not to kill."

She looked up at him. "Which means?"

He shrugged. "It may not mean anything. I don't judge, Springshadow. I merely observe. It's really all I'm competent to do."

Perhaps the strangest — and certainly most annoying — thing about Wildeye was his penchant for stating the truth, even about himself. Strange because he had not achieved his immortality through meditation or the Eight Pillars of Taoist practices. Rather, he had managed to slip into Heaven itself and steal one of the peaches of immortality from the Celestial Garden. He was immortal because he had no choice. He was powerful because it was the nature of power to align itself with immortals of all stripes. He claimed no special virtue, and it's true enough that, so far as Springshadow had observed, he possessed none. He had become Springshadow's friend over the centuries because they understood one another, though sometimes Springshadow ruefully conceded that he understood her just a little too well.

"So I killed one lover rather than hundreds. One life is still a murder, and I

4

am guilty. The fool married me before he died, thus I have murdered my husband and am doubly guilty. As I am never going to die and face judgment from the Lord of the Underworld or anyone else, the consequences don't particularly concern me."

"Spoken like a true fox," said Wildeye with grudging respect. "How long?"

"My One-Thousandth birthday is tomorrow. At dawn I will become an immortal."

"Then I will return to greet the dawn with you. I've never seen this transformation before," said Wildeye, and in a blast of wind and swirl of clouds, he was gone.

"Neither have I," Springshadow said, though she was quite alone.

Her isolation was not quite literally true. Though not yet immortal, she already had the gift of awareness and used it now to scan the terrain surrounding her mountain home. It was, as she expected, nearly empty. That was one reason she had chosen it in the first place. While she had cherished the gift of awareness when it had come to her on her one-hundredth birthday, over the years it had become more a burden than anything. Honestly, why should she care that a nightingale two mountains over thought a particular pebble was very shiny? Such things could fill her mind if she let them, which is why these days she never used her awareness except to check if anyone in the vicinity wished her harm. She had never found anyone who did, since very few people knew who and what she was, and those who did either didn't care, or if wronged, were in no position to seek revenge.

All her careful planning would culminate at tomorrow's dawn, and that, she knew, would be that. She would have succeeded where so many others of her kind had failed. Springshadow only knew of one other fox who had made the transformation, a male known as Sunflash, and no one had seen him in centuries. Some of her kind wondered about this absence and what it meant, but Springshadow did not wonder. A Heavenly Fox would clearly have concerns far beyond those of mortal foxkind. Tomorrow she would know what those concerns were and share them. She would dwell in the Heavens. She would be nothing less than a goddess. Springshadow had never been a goddess before. She could hardly wait to try it.

"Hello," said someone who should not have been there.

Springshadow looked up to find a radiant being in yellow and blue robes smiling down at her. The intruder appeared to be a human woman of surpassing beauty, but Springshadow knew a goddess when she saw one — even though she had never seen one in her long life before this morning. Illusion was second nature to a fox, and Springshadow would have known if the being was something other than what she appeared to be. In an instant Springshadow was on her feet, her weariness forgotten. She put as much distance between herself and the intruder as she reasonably could.

"Who are you?!"

The goddess raised her right hand, palm open and facing toward Springshadow. "I'm sorry if I startled you, but I mean you no harm, Springshadow. My name is Guan Shi Yin."

"The Goddess of Mercy?"

Now Springshadow was really confused. Guan Shi Yin had several special realms of responsibility, including helping infertile women and comforting souls in

5

pain, even those tormented in the pits of hell. Yet there was nothing about her, so far as Springshadow knew, that had any interest in foxes, heavenly or otherwise.

"The same," said the goddess. "My methods of travel are somewhat unconventional, so I didn't realize you wouldn't know that I was coming. Again, my apologies."

Springshadow wasn't sure if she should bow or not, so she settled for a polite nod. "To...to what do I owe the honor of this visit, Immanent One?"

There was a trace of a smile on the goddess's face. At least Springshadow thought there might be. Or perhaps it was just her normal expression.

"Springshadow, tomorrow you will have lived one thousand years as a mortal. Since you are a student of The Den and Burrow Guide to Immortality, I have no doubt that you think you understand what that means, but one effect you may not be aware of is that an impending ascension weakens the barriers between the Heavens and the mortal realm. This allowed me to find you easily. In my capacity as the advocate of the dead, I was asked to deliver a message to you."

This was an eventuality that Springshadow had not prepared for. Apparently her impending ascension had already come to the attention of Heaven. She wasn't entirely sure that this was a good thing. She had spent most of her life avoiding anything that might interfere with her plans. This development had the scent of interference — or worse — all over it.

She steeled herself. "A message? From Whom?"

"In life he was your husband, Zou Xiaofan."

For a moment, Springshadow forgot to breathe. She composed herself with an effort. "You're running errands for a lowly ghost?"

The smile, while remaining ethereal and faint, didn't waver. "My special charge is the ease of suffering. There was something Xiaofan wished to tell you. The matter was troubling him greatly."

"Where is he?" Springshadow asked.

"In one of the numerous and varied hells. Which one is probably of little concern to you. Will you hear his message?"

Springshadow licked her lips. "Must I?"

The goddess shrugged. "You may refuse. Shall I tell him you do not want to hear what he has to say?"

Springshadow finally shook her head. "I am no coward, to be afraid of a mere ghost. You have learned what passed between myself and Xiaofan and I do not deny it. I did what I had to do and would do so again."

"I have accused you of nothing, nor do I intend to do so. I do not judge; that is not my dominion. Will you hear what Xiaofan wished to tell you?"

"I will," Springshadow said. She made an effort to keep her gaze level. "Though it is safe to assume that Xiaofan will accuse me of much. Mostly justified, as I said. No matter. If it will ease Xiaofan's suffering, I am willing to bear the brunt of his hatred. It's the least I can do. What does he say?"

"He wants you to know that he understands why you did what you did. He says that he still loves you."

"Oh," Springshadow said. For a long time, that was all she said. Then she sighed. "What an idiot."

§

Hours later Springshadow and Guan Shi Yin sat together in front of Springshadow's hearth. Somewhat to the fox's surprise, the goddess had gladly accepted a cup of tea, and they had talked so far into the night that it was almost morning.

"It's not that I really expected you to be impressed by Xiaofan's chivalry," Guan Shi Yin said after they had become better acquainted. "You're a fox. And that sort of nobility is easier for humans to both generate and appreciate...no offense intended."

"None taken," Springshadow said. "I suppose it's something like being color-blind. My eyesight as a fox is very keen — I have no problem with shadows and edges, for instance, but I just can't quite get a handle on 'red'."

"Or human feelings?"

Springshadow shrugged. "Those too. The basic motivations are easy enough: hunger, lust, fear, and such. Foxes and humans share those. A lot of the rest of the human perspective is just a mystery to me. Though I daresay I've gotten quite good at mimicking it."

"I dare say," Guan Shi Yin agreed and sipped her tea.

"What do you think Xiaofan was trying to accomplish by this message to me? I mean, honestly? He's dead, he's in hell, and he was placed in a particular hell by the Lord of the Underworld's judgment, so it's reasonable to assume he belongs there. Why should I feel guilty about that?"

The goddess shrugged. "I'm not saying you should. I delivered the message because Xiaofan prayed to me and said that my doing so would ease his suffering, and so I agreed. Easing the suffering of individuals is what I do. I know that, as the Buddha teaches, desire is the root of all such suffering, but I don't pretend to know all the shapes and manifestations that desire takes. Everyone's a little different."

"Would it help him if I asked you to tell him that I love him too? And that I'm sorry for what I did to him?"

"Is either true?"

Springshadow thought about it. "I don't think so. I had some affection for Xiaofan, but I killed him to get what I needed, which does not sound like love to me. As for the second, definitely not."

"Then I can't deliver that message," Guan Shi Yin said, and this time Springshadow was sure that the goddess was smiling, if ever so faintly. "I can neither lie nor knowingly carry a lie. A not always convenient virtue, I'll grant you."

Springshadow shrugged. "Well, then. It was just a thought."

Outside her mountain cave the sky was turning pale. Springshadow rose and walked out to the cave entrance, Guan Shi Yin following. The dawn sky was just visible as a yellow-orange streak to the east, a streak that was growing wider and brighter and coming closer by the moment.

"It's almost time. How do you feel?" the goddess asked.

7

"I feel...expansive," Springshadow said. "Like there's more to me than I thought there was."

"I'd say your spirit is preparing itself. Ah, that will be Wildeye."

The wild-haired Taoist roared up on his golden cloud, disturbing the sound of the morning birds. He hopped off onto the broad ledge in front of Springshadow's cave, while his cloud flitted up to circle the mountain peak, idly. "Sorry I'm late. Have I missed anything?"

"Much," said Guan Shi Yin, "but if you're referring to Springshadow's apotheosis, you're still on time."

Wildeye looked as if he wanted to go back the way he'd come when he saw Guan Shi Yin, but he merely spared a grudging and hasty bow in the goddess's general direction and went up to Springshadow. "It won't be long now."

The first direct glimmer of the sun was visible over the mountains. For a moment Springshadow gazed in wonder as its glow enveloped her, before she realized that glow was not a reflection of the sun but was arising from within herself. She stared at her hands, now glowing like molten bronze in a furnace.

"I-I can't contain it!"

The expansive feeling she had before was nothing compared to this. She felt at once like Springshadow greeting the dawn on her One-Thousandth Birthday and the dawn itself, spreading to encompass the world and everything around it. She was Springshadow, and yet she was also Guan Shi Yin and Wildeye, and a hermit on the next mountain dreaming of a woman, and an immortal two mountains over from that who was not dreaming of anything. She was all those things and becoming more all the time. She was exhilarated. She was terrified.

Somewhere in the distance she felt a touch on her shoulder and knew it was Guan Shi Yin, because she herself was Guan Shi Yin, or the other way round, and every other way there was.

"You're just touching the Universal Truth," said the goddess's voice, at once distant and yet more intimate than a whisper. "You won't forget, but you'll stop dwelling on it after a while. Helps one to function. Even a goddess."

"What Universal Truth?" Springshadow asked, but even as she asked, she knew. There was no Guan Shi Yin, no Wildeye, no hermit two mountains over or an immortal on the next peak. They were all the same thing. Everything and everyone, aware or not, was the same thing. And, for that moment, Springshadow was that everything, all that was or would be. Just before she felt that surely she would succumb to that knowledge and become everything forever, she felt another hand on her other shoulder. That was Wildeye.

"Time to come down, girl."

It was like a bucket of cold water in the face. Springshadow felt herself shrinking down like a doused fire until she stood on the mountain ledge and was just Springshadow again. But that other knowledge, that other awareness and certainty, was still there, like a letter locked in a box that she could read at any time and call back everything that the letter evoked. She felt a little dizzy.

"That wasn't very nice," Guan Shi Yin said.

Disoriented as she was, it was a moment or two before she realized that Guan

Shi Yin and Wildeye were arguing. "She touched the Universal Truth and was this close," Guan Shi Yin held her two index fingers barely a whisker's width apart, "to transcending. And you had to spoil it!"

"And watch my friend fall into that trap of oblivion? Not a chance, Immanence."

Springshadow groaned and found a convenient rock to sit down on. It was a familiar rock, one she had used to take the evening air on countless occasions. But it felt different to her now, somehow...wrong. She tried to focus on the two squabbling immortals. "What are you two going on about?"

It occurred to Springshadow that she could know exactly what they were squabbling about. She had the key. She decided that, for now, it was simpler merely to ask.

"Part of the process of apotheosis is an introduction to transcendence. Some choose to remain in that state," Guan Shi Yin said. "It looked like you had chosen that path when this oaf intervened."

"And who was it had her hand on the girl's other shoulder? Your contact had as much to do with her return as mine."

"At least I didn't call her back."

"No, but you do want her back. You want her as she is now! Don't bother to deny it," Wildeye said. "You know you can't lie to me. You can't lie to anyone."

Guan Shi Yin scowled at him but finally sighed. "It's true. I need her."

"For what?" Springshadow asked. "And what the heck is wrong with my rock? If feels like its grown a knot."

"That's not the rock, girl. That's you," Wildeye said. "Stand up."

Springshadow stood up. Her form was somewhere between fully human and fully vulpine; a transitional form that gave her human hands and other aspects of humans that were useful, without fully surrendering her fox senses, and she'd used it often. Only now there seemed to be more to it. Several "mores", actually. "My tail feels funny."

"Say rather your tails, girl," Wildeye said, and started counting.

"You're a Heavenly Fox now, Springshadow. Look up," said the goddess.

Springshadow looked up. There, in the distant sky far beyond the clouds, far beyond the mortal world yet clearly visible, clearly reachable, was a magnificent floating city with towers of gold and walls of the finest jade.

Wildeye gave a grunt of triumph as he finished his count. "Nine! And each as magnificent as the last."

"What are you babbling about? Nine what?" Springshadow said, unable for the moment to take her eyes off of Heaven and the floating city.

"Tails, of course," he said. "Yours."

That finally got Springshadow's attention. She quickly glanced behind her like a courtesan checking her appearance. It took her a moment to understand what she was seeing, but she finally saw what Wildeye saw — fox tails.

Nine in all, and all, as Wildeye said, belonging to her. Attached.

"Nine?!"

"Nine." Wildeye nodded in grudging respect. "You have to admit," he said to the goddess, "that's pretty damn impressive."

Part 2: To Discover the Question

It was the sight of the multiple tails that finally pulled Springshadow's attention off the City of Heaven. "Nine what?!"

"Tails," Guan Shi Yin said. "Don't tell me you didn't know about that part? A Heavenly Fox grows extra tails as an indicator of the level of their spiritual powers. At least one extra, often more. Nine is, as Wildeye pointed out, very impressive."

"Why would I want extra tails? The one I had was quite good enough!"

Wildeye shook his head. "It's not a question of wanting them, girl! You're a Heavenly Fox, so now you have them. That's the beginning and end of it."

Springshadow, when she paused to consider the matter, realized it was very silly to dwell on the fact that she had nine tails, considering what had just happened to her. And yet it was hard not to do that very thing. With all nine fanning out behind her, she felt more like a peacock than a fox. On an impulse she transformed into her full human female appearance, and was somewhat relieved to see that her multitude of tails also vanished, along with the rest of her vulpine attributes.

"At least I can transform into a human if I want to sit down."

Wildeye frowned. "And if you remained purely fox, you wouldn't need to sit down. You could curl up like an honest fox, tails and all. Really, girl, why do you insist on being neither one thing nor another?"

Springshadow scowled. "I'm an immortal now. I'm not feeling inclined to accept limitations. I think I'll go experience the world as an immortal. My world now, as an immortal, including Heaven."

"Do what you think you must," Guan Shi Yin said. "Then come see me when you are ready to be serious."

"What are you talking about?" Springshadow asked, but the goddess had already disappeared, winking out like a candle flame but not even leaving so much as a wisp of smoke behind.

"I'd watch out for that one, if I were you," Wildeye said.

Springshadow frowned. "The Goddess of Mercy? Of all the immortals in the heavens, I'd think she would be the one least likely to intend harm to anyone."

"Intend? No. But all immortals have their own spheres and their own purposes, and the Goddess of Mercy is no different. More, she wants something from you. She said as much."

Springshadow frowned again. "She also said that I should 'go see her when I was ready to be serious'. What does that mean?"

Wildeye scratched under his beard, looking thoughtful. "I don't know. She does not lie, but she can keep silent when it suits her, and what she hasn't said echoes like thunder to me. Where thunder is, there you'll find lightning often as not."

Springshadow shook her head. "I went through all that I have gone through, done all I have done, so that I would never have to worry about anything ever again, and I'm not going to spoil that by fretting about Guan Shi Yin. There's nothing she can do to me. There's nothing anyone can do to me."

Springshadow stepped to the edge of the mountain ledge. "And since I'm an Immortal like you, I want a cloud like yours."

Ever since the age of five hundred, Springshadow had known the trick of conjuring a small white cloud that could bear her weight when she needed to travel far and swiftly. Now that same cloud had developed a golden tint, identical to Wildeye's. When she summoned it, the newly golden cloud floated up even with the top of the ledge, purring like a cat.

"It's an aspect of being Immortal," Wildeye said. "All you had to do was ask. Now what?"

"Now I am going to take a closer look at Heaven. Do you wish to come?"

He sighed. "I'm not exactly welcome in the Jade Realm these days. But you go. Have fun."

"I intend to."

Springshadow stepped onto her eager cloud and soared up to Heaven, higher than she had ever gone before. As she was just getting used to the changes in herself, it took her a moment longer to realize how much her cloud had changed as well. Where before its cloud-nature made the silly thing extremely reluctant to rise above the other, non-magical clouds that dotted the sky, now it leapt past those timid wisps of vapor like an arrow grazing a flock of geese and left them far below in seconds.

What had been impossibly distant, out of sight, out of bounds, was now spread open before Springshadow like a scroll she couldn't wait to read. Heaven seemed incredibly vast, even for someone used to traveling by flying cloud, but it was no longer impossible. She saw a city with palaces and walls of jade, people of serene countenance and perfection going about their business just as they would in any other city. Granted, some of the denizens appeared a bit strange, but so far she saw nothing she had not seen before at various times in the Middle Kingdom of Earth: dragons, Qilin, gods, goddesses, sages, students and scholars of various ranks from high to low, kings and queens.

Springshadow enjoyed the sight of all this for a long time, but eventually the mere act of seeing Heaven wasn't enough. She had to become part of it, as was her right. She ordered her cloud, now flying higher than the Jade City itself, to descend. Springshadow landed on a broad, pristine street on her golden cloud, and since this was the Jade City, no one took any notice of her. So much so that as one portly man wearing scholar's robes came rushing down the street, he practically collided with her, and it was only her nimble fox reflexes that prevented it.

"Please excuse me," he said, though his voice was already fading in the distance. He hadn't even broken stride.

Springshadow frowned. "What was — "

She didn't get to finish as another man in scholar's robes, somewhat taller and slimmer than the first but otherwise very much like him, came hurrying down the street. Springshadow was careful to stay out of this one's path, but she reached out quickly as the man passed and tapped him on the shoulder.

"Excuse me?" she said, but the man was already three paces past her before he managed to stop.

"Yes, what is it?" he asked, looking rather distracted.

"Pardon my ignorance, but where are you going in such a hurry? What could be so pressing in this place?"

For a moment the man simply stared at her as if she had just grown an extra head. "Pressing? Why, the Official Examinations, of course! This will be my third attempt to qualify as Scholar, Second Level."

"That sounds exciting, and I hope you succeed," Springshadow said. "But what then?"

"Why, the studies and exam for Scholar, First Level, of course."

She blinked. "And then? What will you do?"

"There are always the advanced grades, such as Order of the Red Quill for composition, the Auditors for Special Merit, the Fellowship of the Jade Tablet, the — "

"Yes, yes," Springshadow interrupted, "I mean, what will you do once your examinations are completed? What is your ultimate purpose? What do you want to do?"

He seemed to consider the question somewhat ridiculous. "The exams are never completed. There is always another level, something new to aspire to. Now if you'll excuse me, I mustn't be late." In a moment he was hurrying down the street again, wide sleeves flapping behind him in a breeze of his own making. Soon he was lost even to Springshadow's keen sight.

"That was very strange," she said aloud and to no one in particular.

Yet, upon reflection, Springshadow realized it was not really so odd as all that. After all, Xiaofan had been such a scholar, studying for the official examinations. Granted, a scholar's place and prospects in the Middle Kingdom had always depended on how well they did on a series of official examinations, but there were limits. At least, Springshadow had believed there were such, even though sometimes it seemed to her, even then, that Xiaofan was more intent on the examinations themselves than the purpose behind them. Which, Springshadow had always believed, was to better oneself. That was no more or less than what she herself had wanted, in the process of becoming a Heavenly Fox. Perhaps the people of the Jade City had a different perspective.

"If so, then why are they doing the exact same things?"

Springshadow didn't get an answer from the denizens of the Jade City itself. She saw them coming and going on the same street. Her surroundings were strange and wondrous, and yet familiar, all at the same time. If the streets were of alabaster and the walls of the compounds and the walls of the palaces were all of jade, the construction techniques were no different, if more refined, from what she was used

13

to seeing on the streets of the capital.

"This is all wrong."

In an instant Guan Shi Yin was standing by her side. "Really? What did you expect?"

"Paradise!" Springshadow said. "Isn't that what Heaven is?"

"This is it," the goddess said. "Isn't it marvelous?"

"Well, of course. But why is it the same? I mean, so much like the Middle Kingdom?"

"What should it be?" the goddess asked.

"Different," Springshadow said.

"So you're saying that paradise should be something other than a comfortable place where people enjoy the bliss of their higher natures?"

"Yes! No! I don't know. It's just that, well, I don't know what I expected or wanted, exactly. I simply know that this isn't it."

Guan Shi Yin raised an eyebrow. "I must say you discovered the question far sooner than I thought likely, even for a fox."

Springshadow blinked. "What question? And why 'for a fox'?"

"The 'Is Heaven All There Is?' question. Though it's not really a question. The only reason anyone has the sense to ask it in the first place is because they already know that the answer is 'no'. And as 'for a fox', it's just that, being an animal, your mind works differently than a human's. Human beings tend to see, not themselves, but an idea of themselves. What they think they are or pretend they are or want to be. For such beings, such a place like this is paradise. They take what they find here and work out a way to fit their idea of themselves into it, so how can it be any less than what they expect?"

Springshadow sighed gustily. "Pardon me, Immanence, but I didn't understand half of that."

"Good. It's smoke and mirrors to a fox anyway. You know what you are. You know what you see. And after less than an hour within the gates of the Jade City, you're confused and disappointed. As I said: quick. Sunflash took a full week."

Sunflash. Springshadow was familiar with the name, of course. He was a legend among fox kind, one of the first to prove that what Springshadow had been taught as a kit was true, that foxes could achieve the state of Heavenly Foxes. He had not been seen in the Middle Kingdom for centuries, but Springshadow's attention wasn't really on him at the moment.

Springshadow sighed. "You're saying that Heaven is not for the likes of me."

Guan Shi Yin smiled. "Yes, I am saying exactly that. Yet you're still new enough at being an Immortal that you think this is a bad thing, some failing in you. Quite the opposite, I'd say. Heaven can be as much a trap as any hell."

"Why didn't you warn me?"

"Because you wouldn't believe me. Now your understanding has already progressed beyond this place."

"But I don't understand! Does this have anything to do with that feeling I had when I first transformed? That I was everyone? That everyone was me?"

"You know it does."

"But what does it mean?"

Guan Shi Yin smiled again, and despite the goddess's reputation for compassion, Springshadow did not think it a very kind smile. It was more the smile she herself might have worn just before eating a particularly tasty bit of meat.

"That's the second question. And you'll have to work for the answer to that one," the goddess said.

Springshadow was quiet for a while. She finally turned to the goddess and said, "I won't do it."

"Do what?"

"Whatever it is you want me to do. I won't."

"Without even knowing what it is? Why not?"

"Why should I? I'm an immortal. Why should I accept obligations?"

Guan Shi Yin smiled that same disturbing smile. "No reason. Unless..."

Springshadow frowned. "Unless what?"

"Unless in, say, another thousand years, you can think of a reason."

The goddess disappeared again. Springshadow wasn't sure if she should be relieved or not, but either way she was alone again, except for all the multitudes of the Jade City. Springshadow felt very much alone indeed.

For want of a better plan, Springshadow ascended on her cloud again and explored the Celestial City from above. It was, as before, both familiar and new, and so grand and vast and fine that, at least for a while, she was able to forget her disappointment. Her fox nature found her looking for something green that was not simply jade, and after a while she found it — an open park near the center of the city, with trees and grass and many separate, wondrous gardens with birds and flowers in abundance.

Springshadow bade her cloud to take her to the park, and it settled her in a secluded place near benches of marble, fine woods, and jade. For a little while Springshadow resumed her true fox form, contemplating a little sport hunting mice and bugs under the trees and flowers, but whenever she tried to slip quietly through the undergrowth and bushes she found that her nine tails flared out behind her almost like the broad tail of a peacock, and brushed limbs, dislodged petals, and basically rendered the idea of moving quietly anywhere except the open areas completely moot.

"What use are nine tails to a fox?!" she demanded of the universe, not really expecting an answer. She got one anyway.

"You're no longer a simple fox, Immortal One. Forgive my impertinence, but I thought that was the point." The voice was low-pitched and male, but Springshadow saw nothing and smelled only earth and green growing things.

She looked around. "Who said that?"

"I did."

Springshadow used her sensitive ears to get a better bearing on the voice,

15

and once she had a direction, she finally spotted the one who spoke. He was a small man dressed in green robes that blended almost perfectly into the hedge he stood against. He carried a short staff, and his head was large compared to his body.

"I'm sorry, I didn't see you, Honored Sir. To whom am I speaking?"

"My name is Hsien Se. This is my garden."

"I am sorry. I didn't mean to trespass."

He smiled. "Not at all. When I say that this is my garden, I meant rather that I am responsible for it. The garden belongs to the Jade Emperor, who has decreed that it be open to everyone, so that all the inhabitants of the Celestial City may enjoy it. What do you think of my garden?"

"It's beautiful. I have never seen a finer one," Springshadow said, and it was the truth.

"Thank you. One does try to take pride in one's work."

Springshadow frowned. The man's name was familiar. It finally came to her. "You are a god of plants and growing things, are you not?"

"I am. I have duties back in the Middle Kingdom as well as here. It does keep one busy." The man's staff transformed into a scythe, which he used to trim a weed from a bed of peonies. In even less than a blink of an eye, the scythe was a simple staff again. Hsien Se leaned on that staff as he studied his handiwork and finally nodded. "It was its own fault, you know. I warned that dandelion not to grow there. I keep telling it, 'a weed is simply a flower that grows out of its place'. It never listens. Tomorrow I'll have to trim it again. Oh, where are my manners? There's a bench here. Please sit and rest yourself."

Springshadow transformed herself into a human girl again, to take advantage of Hsien Se's kind offer, but it took her a little more effort to get all nine of her tails to disappear. Even so, her human form was the only one where her extra appendages seemed manageable. "I'm starting to feel a bit like a weed myself," Springshadow said, as she finally managed to sit down.

"You're newly immortal. I can tell. It does take some adjustment."

"How did you adjust? If it's not impolite to ask."

"Not at all, but I'm afraid my experience might not be of any use to you."

"Why not?"

"Because it doesn't have much resemblance to your own. You are a fox, correct? You achieved immortality by living for one thousand years of mortal time? I would guess that you expended a great deal of effort and sacrifice to achieve this?"

"Yes," Springshadow said, "though in honesty not all the sacrifices were my own."

"That's as may be. I, on the other hand, was given very little say in the matter. In the Middle Kingdom, I began my existence as a peasant farmer. My sole distinction was that I was a very skilled farmer. Others came to me for advice, which they often followed to their advantage. When I died, those who knew me began to pray to my spirit for the same sort of aid. Soon people who didn't even know me were doing the same. Do you have any idea what that sort of prayer and reverence does to a human spirit after a while?"

16

Springshadow admitted that she did not. Hsien Se nodded and went on, "That sort of reverence empowers one, like it or not. My inclination was to help, and so, when I was able, I did help. My surviving family at first, but as my power increased so did my sphere of action. Now in certain cults only kings and emperors are allowed to sacrifice to me directly. Not bad for a peasant farmer from Shaodong, true, but mostly the matter was out of my hands. I became a god of agriculture because a god was needed. No one asked me if I wanted the position."

"But I'm not a goddess. In my early ignorance, I thought I would become one," Springshadow said, and Hsien Se smiled.

"My point, Lady. You are immortal, true, but in order to be a goddess, you would have to be a goddess of something. A god or goddess has a sphere of influence and responsibility. You do not have such, and I sense that you don't really want one. You are free in ways that one such as myself or the Jade Emperor can never be. In some respects I envy you."

"But what do I do?" Springshadow asked.

"Anything you want. In that I do not envy you at all."

"I don't understand," Springshadow said, even though her fear was that she did understand, and all too perfectly.

Hsien Se sighed. "Without me, this garden would suffer, so I choose what is best for it with the understanding that my choices have consequences. If you can do anything you want without consequence, then nothing depends on what you do, so one choice is as good as another. If that's so, then why does anything you do matter?"

"It doesn't, does it?"

"No, except perhaps in one instance."

"What's that?"

"If the choice matters to you. What matters to you, Lady?"

"I don't know," Springshadow said, and the god nodded.

"That's why I don't envy you. Sunflash had the same problem."

Springshadow blinked. "You know Sunflash? What did he do in this situation?"

"I can't say for sure. He has not been in the Celestial City for ages. He used to come to my garden quite a bit to play with the mice."

Springshadow blushed slightly, remembering one of her own reasons for coming to the garden. "Do you know where he is now?"

"I'm afraid not. Why?"

"You said it yourself, Honored Sir — he had the same problem I do. Assuming he hasn't gone insane and destroyed himself, then he's found an answer. An answer, perhaps, he will share with me."

Hsien Se sighed. "I do suppose it's possible, though if his absence from the city is any indication, his answer was not to be found here."

Springshadow smiled her brightest smile. "If I might impose on your kindness for one more question?"

17

"Certainly."

"You don't know where he is. Do you know who might?"

"The Master of the Hall of Records. There are few matters so insignificant that he would not have some reference to them. Including the location of one elusive fox, I would wager. To find the Hall of Records, fly due west of the Jade Palace for no more than a league. The Hall will be the huge building that resembles a beehive."

Springshadow thanked Hsien Se and recalled her golden cloud. She flew away from the garden leaving the farming god happily pruning the plum trees with his magic scythe.

§

Springshadow followed Hsian Se's directions and found the Hall of Records within minutes. As Springshadow considered the size of the Celestial City, it occurred to her that the Hall of Records must have an important function indeed to be located so near the Jade Palace of the King of Heaven. The Hall itself was exactly as described: a towering bell-shaped edifice with what looked like thousands of separate doors, all in constant use. Just before she descended, Springshadow enhanced her appearance a bit and now wore the form of a Heavenly Maiden, one of the multitudes of sylphs and angelic beings that inhabited the Celestial City. She found a door that seemed no more or less busy than all the others and entered the Hall.

The clerks in the Celestial Hall of Records didn't look like what Springshadow had come to expect from xiān , as the inhabitants of the Celestial City were sometimes known. In fact, there was something of the demonic about them. Or maybe it was just the fact that they moved so fast, like ants. She soon realized that her disguise as a Heavenly Maiden was a wasted effort. The clerks took no notice of her at all, except to detour around her as necessary, as a stream flowed around a stone or any other obstacle, heedless of its nature except as obstacle.

The Hall itself was every bit as vast as she had expected and consisted of little save one vast open space containing walls filled to every available surface with cubbyholes or ramps and ladders from the multitude of doors. Each cubbyhole had one or more scrolls placed within. The clerks' function seemed to be to snatch a scroll from its cubby, unroll it long enough to write something with brushes that never seemed to run out of ink, then put the scroll back where it belonged. As a Heavenly Fox, Springshadow had the ability to know what was going on around her, and she used that skill on the clerks and the Hall.

It's too much too much too much!

While her ability worked well enough on earth, in this place it was stretched to the limit of her sanity. It was as if billions of voices were speaking at once, and for that instant, she understood and could identify and follow every one. It was too much. She shut them out as quickly as she could, but the experience left her shaken. Even so, out of all the nearly infinite voices, she had been able to ascertain one of use to her: the person in charge. Springshadow moved quickly through the Hall, and in the distance, could just make out a figure seated in state against the far wall.

He was an imposing creature perhaps nine feet tall, a mandarin with a grotesque face and a black lacquered hat and rich brocade robes of red and yellow.

18

Unlike the clerks, he was barely moving at all, save when one would scurry up to him, bow, ask a question and be answered, then scurry away again. Springshadow bowed in turn as she approached.

"Forgive me, Illustrious Sir, but I was wondering if you could tell me — "

"You!" shouted the seated figure, as if he hadn't heard a word she'd said. He pointed into the throng, and in an instant one of the scurrying clerks detached itself from the seething mass that was the rest of the clerks and approached the throne, for such Springshadow took it to be.

"Bring me the current scroll on the fox named Springshadow," he said.

The clerk shot away and then hurried back, bearing a large scroll that he gave to the mandarin sitting there, who immediately unrolled it and began studying it closely.

"You're looking for the fox named Sunflash, it says here."

Springshadow was so startled that it was several moments before she realized the demon, god, man, or whatever it was, was indeed speaking to her.

"Yes...yes, Honored Sir. How did you know that?"

He frowned. "I'm the Master of the Hall of Records, and the information is in your record, of course. Everything's written there, or how else could one keep track?"

Springshadow blinked. "Everything?"

"Right down to the grasshoppers you ate when you were a kit. Whose tiny souls still cry for vengeance, by the way."

Springshadow had a sudden vision of every creature she had eaten appearing at her own judgment as witnesses for the prosecution. She felt a little dizzy, which the man on his throne apparently noticed. "Don't worry. The creatures you ate were in turn paying for actions in their own previous lives. As your eating them was part of their karmic obligations, they won't count against you. Though they still do complain."

"But is it really necessary to record everything?"

"When a person dies, that person's soul goes to judgment. If Lord Yama, King of the Dead who judges the dead does not have proper records, how can any soul be judged correctly?"

"But I'm immortal now!"

"Which means that your record will be much longer, exceeding one scroll. More work for me. Fortunately, except for the citizens of the Celestial City, there are not so very many of your sort. Now then, to business — Guan Shi Yin has asked that I show you consideration, and so I shall."

"She read my scroll, too?"

"The Goddess of Mercy knows what is necessary for her to know, within her sphere of concern. I had nothing to do with it."

"Why would she want to help me?"

"I cannot say unless I pull her scroll, and as that annoys her, I try not to do it. As a general rule she's concerned with everyone. It's what she does. Now then

— you wish to know where the Heavenly Fox known as Sunflash can be found?"

Springshadow decided she just wouldn't think about what the Master of the Hall of Records was telling her. It was too confusing, and she was having enough trouble keeping her mind on her goal. "Yes, please. Is he alive? Where is he?"

"You!" shouted the Master of the Hall of Records, and pointed again. Within moments yet another scroll — a very long one — had been presented to the mandarin, who glanced at it and replied, "Yes, Sunflash is still alive. He is currently in the Hell of Hungry Ghosts."

"The Hell...?"

"Of Hungry Ghosts. Yes."

"If he's alive, what is he doing in that hell or any other?"

The Master of the Hall of Records frowned. "That is actually a good question. I'd like to know the answer myself." He studied the document again, and for the first time since she'd approached him, he smiled. "Interesting."

Springshadow found her patience wearing thin. "No doubt, but will you share this interesting information?"

"It says here that he's gone to the Hell of Hungry Ghosts to wait."

"For what?"

"For you."

Part 3: To Find at Least One Answer

Springshadow entered the Hell of Hungry Ghosts under the guise of Guan Shi Yin. She shone with a golden light and wore robes of purest white.

"That disguise is not necessary, you know," said a voice beside her. "No one here cares who you are."

For a moment Springshadow thought she was looking into a very tall mirror. Then she realized the real Guan Shi Yin was standing beside her, looking amused. Springshadow returned to her true fox form, nine tails and all, and bowed her muzzle to the goddess. "Please forgive me. I wasn't certain about the protocol for entering a Hell one wasn't condemned to."

The goddess shrugged. "It's done all the time. Those who have to be here are here. As are those who choose to be. The difference is simply how soon one can leave. Though I really think you should give some introspection as to why your first instinct is to appear to be something you're not."

Despite her embarrassment, Springshadow did think about what the goddess said. "Perhaps because I'm not certain who I am."

"You are a Heavenly Fox," the goddess said.

"Yes, but what is that? And by the way, when we first met, you said there was something you wanted me to do. What is that?"

Guan Shi Yin smiled. "You've learned to ask the right questions. It's a start. So. I have business here, and it seems, so do you. Perhaps we'll talk later about that other matter."

The goddess disappeared, leaving Springshadow alone on what appeared to be a road of hard stone and gravel. The Hell of Hungry Ghosts was a bleak place, with coarse sand and spires of rock. It was neither particularly hot nor particularly cold. Springshadow looked around her, puzzled.

"What is the punishment?"

There was no one around to answer her. Other than Guan Shi Yin, she had seen no one since her arrival. Her little golden cloud had been too frightened to follow her into the hell, so Springshadow was reduced to walking if she wished to get anywhere at all. She continued down the road for want of a better direction.

In time she did begin to see others. She hesitated to call them "people", as there didn't seem to be much about them that was a person, as she understood the term. Their shapes were oddly changed. One man had enormous hands and no mouth. Another had large ears but no eyes. A woman crawled on four stubs and had neither eyes nor mouth, only a large nose, which she ran along the ground like a hound sniffing for a spoor. All seemed to be searching for something, and those who had mouths and tongues to form sounds would occasionally emit a low moan or a wail or a shriek, but for no apparent reason.

Springshadow understood that the denizens of the Hell of Hungry Ghosts were being deprived, but of exactly what she wasn't sure. Perhaps everything. To call the place thoroughly unpleasant hardly did it justice, but mostly she found it puzzling.

"Why would Sunflash come to this wretched place?"

The Hell of Hungry Ghosts was clearly a vast domain, and without her little golden cloud, Springshadow could not cover a great deal of distance quickly, even as a fox. She considered that she might be weeks, months, or years walking along this hard, stony road. And then Guan Shi Yin was walking beside her again as if she had never left.

"It seems our business here is with the same person."

"Sunflash? Do you know where he is?"

"The same, and of course I do. I know where every denizen of every hell is, or else how could I find them when their time has come to leave?"

Springshadow bowed. "Please, Your Immanence, would you take me to him?"

"Would I? I actually insist upon it. He's being very stubborn."

Springshadow smiled. "Ah. I knew you wanted something from me, back when I first transformed from a mortal fox. So this is what that was all about."

"Actually it is Sunflash who wants something from you. And speaking of transforming, would you mind taking human form again? It might make things easier."

Springshadow quickly changed back into a young woman, but she did not look like Guan Shi Yin this time. She took the appearance of the girl Xiaofan had loved, and the Goddess of Mercy took her by the hand. In an instant the landscape was flashing past them in one great blur. Springshadow had the strange feeling that the hell itself was moving, parting around them just as the clerks in the Hall of Records moved to accommodate a foreign presence. In another moment the shifting terrain slowed, then stopped. The two women stood beside a clump of the sort of stone spires that Springshadow had noticed earlier. The spires almost looked like a small mountain range, though their tops were sharper and more pointed than any mountains Springshadow had ever seen. Springshadow was still trying to catch her breath after the sudden shift, but Guan Shi Yin put her hands on her hips and was staring at a narrow defile between two of the spires.

"He's in there. He's waiting for you."

"That's what the Master of the Hall of Records said. Why would he be waiting for me?"

The goddess just sighed. "I think it's best that you ask him that yourself. It's time for him to leave this place, but he refused to budge until he spoke with you. I'd consider it a personal favor if you can reason with him."

"I'll try," Springshadow said, even though she felt much too confused to be reasoning with anyone. She'd sought out Sunflash's guidance only to discover that he'd locked himself away in the Hell of Hungry Ghosts, apparently of his own volition. Now Guan Shi Yin said it was time for him to leave? If he was here by choice, how could there be a set time? She considered questioning the goddess further, but the person she really wanted answers from was waiting for her in a narrow valley somewhere in the Hell of Hungry Ghosts.

She left Guan Shi Yin and entered the valley, though it was little more than a large crack between two dark granite spires. Every now and then she passed one of the creatures who lived there, all of them misshapen, all searching. One or two of them sniffed at her, and she hurried on, out of their reach. Soon she came to a place where the crack widened into something the size of a great hall with sheer stone walls that arched inward, almost meeting overhead like a roof. The interior was shadowed but somehow illuminated from within.

Springshadow hesitated, but finally shook her head. "I've come too far to turn back now."

Springshadow entered the grotto, keeping a close watch for hungry ghosts, but as far as she could tell, she was alone. She followed the light until she realized that it emanated from a lone figure sitting on a large bench of stone. He was in human form and wearing the rich brocade robes of a mandarin, but Springshadow was too familiar with transformation and appearances to be fooled. He was a fox.

He was Sunflash.

"It's certainly about time you arrived," he said as she came into his view. "You kept me waiting so long I was beginning to wonder if you were coming."

She approached cautiously until she was no more than a few feet from where he sat. "How did you know I was coming?"

He smiled. Even in human form he was handsome. Springshadow forced herself to concentrate on the business at hand. So did Sunflash.

"I knew that someone would come, sooner or later. Just as the fox who came before me did. His name was Summerstorm, by the way. Splendid fellow, but I don't suppose you'll have heard of him. No?" Springshadow shook her head and Sunflash went on, "He waited a lot longer than I did, so I really shouldn't complain. Anyway, when my time was getting short, I consulted the Master of the Hall of Records and found that another fox named Springshadow was a mere hundred years away from achieving my status. That's how I knew you were coming."

Springshadow sighed. "My name is Springshadow, but I don't understand any of this. I came to ask you — "

"How to be a Heavenly Fox? And don't ask how I know. That's what I asked Summerstorm. If you'd asked anything else I'd have known you weren't what you appear to be... underneath the transformation, I mean."

"I'm most certainly a fox!"

Sunflash grinned. "And a lovely one, too. Definitely worth waiting for."

Springshadow ignored that. "Guan Shi Yin says you're supposed to leave and won't. Why?"

"Because I was waiting for you, of course. The hundred years was easy enough to measure, but how long before you got the notion to seek me out? No way to predict that. So I extended my time here. It's always easier to find someone who stays put, in my experience."

"But why? What do you want of me?"

He shook his head, smiling again. "You don't understand. I'm here because you want something from me. Like Summerstorm before me, I've chosen to give it. Maybe one day you'll make the same choice. Perhaps not. That's up to you."

"You're telling me you came to the Hell of Hungry Ghosts simply to wait for me?!"

He laughed then. It was a few moments before he could go on while Springshadow, human-like, felt the blood rushing to her face.

"I'm sorry," Sunflash said. "That was rude, but I couldn't help it. No, of course I didn't come here to wait for you. I could have done that anywhere. I was here because I was taking someone's place. Perhaps Her Immanence can explain it better than I."

It was only then that Springshadow noticed that Guan Shi Yin had followed her into the grotto. Her appearance had changed somewhat from before. Now she looked taller, even more splendid. When they had traveled the stony road together, Guan Shi Yin was about the same size as Springshadow. Now the goddess's height, as compared to the foxes', was roughly that of a mother's next to her small children.

"When Sunflash was working toward perfecting the Golden Elixir, he hurt a great many people, just as you did," Guan Shi Yin said. "Over the centuries since then he's been atoning."

Springshadow blinked. "Atoning? Why?"

Sunflash sighed. "I created my potion of immortality the same way you did, by stealing the energy of living mortals. Several died as a result. The last of them was a woman who, for her mistakes in life — myself included, was sentenced to the Hell of Hungry Ghosts. I've since taken her place, and I have been here for the span of time she would have lived had I not bewitched her. She was returned to the living and so given a second chance. That was how I repaid my debt to her. I have repaid my other debts as well, in various ways. As I said: she was the last."

"I still don't understand. What atonement? What debts? We are what we are. The Master of the Hall of Records said I was not to blame for the crickets I ate to stay alive as a kit. If you're going to argue that humans are more than crickets, I would say that the difference is degree, not kind. Why should you or I be blamed for doing what is a fox's nature to do?"

"You shouldn't," Guan Shi Yin said. "In a sense the flaws within those mortals called to you, just as the struggles of an injured fish summons a larger fish. You are blameless in their deaths."

"Then I owe them nothing!"

Guan Shi Yin shook her head, obviously amused. "That's not what I said. I said you were blameless: that is, you're not a murderer. Well may you speak of a fox's nature, but know that the universe has a nature as well, and that is to strive for balance and order. Balance requires that debts be repaid, and you owe value for what you took. Just as Sunflash did, and just as the immortal you know as Wildeye does. You own your debt, so only you can repay it and would do so in your next life, or as many as it takes. That's the Law of Karma which all creatures obey, even the gods."

"But I..."

"Am Immortal, yes," Sunflash said. "Though the term 'immortal' is misleading. Not even the xiān truly live forever incarnate. If we live a long time, that means our debts go unpaid for a very long time. However, karmic debts can only be delayed, not forgiven. Sooner or later, they come due. So I decided not to wait. Guan

24

Shi Yin, as is her own nature, was kind enough to assist me."

"But the thousand years! All that struggle, all that time!"

He grinned. "And, like me, I wager you never once thought to ask yourself what it was for, did you? Or perhaps you thought the ideas of communing with Heaven and achieving immortality and power were enough? I did. I learned better, as apparently did you, or you wouldn't have come looking for me."

"It's not my fault Heaven turned out to be such a boring place!" Springshadow said.

"Why do you think I spend so little time there?" Guan Shi Yin asked, smiling again. "Plus, it's a trap in its own way. Too many people confuse it for the goal, as you did. Even the gods make that mistake sometimes."

"But what is the goal then?"

"Something different," said Guan Shi Yin.

"You're throwing my own words back at me!"

"No, I'm confirming what you already suspect: all you've managed to do with the Golden Elixir and all that stolen life force is to trap yourself in some minor eddy of eternity. Nothing will change, and tomorrow will be just like today, for as close to forever as is worth mentioning. Was that what you hoped to gain when you bewitched those mortals?"

"No," she said.

"What, then?" asked Sunflash.

"I don't know!"

"Neither did I nor do I," Sunflash said. "Even after all this wasted time. I'm sorry, but that's why I've chosen to keep looking. That is my purpose now." He turned to the goddess. "She was my last debt. Is it so?"

Guan Shi Yin smiled. "It is so. I'm ready when you are."

"Then let's be off."

"Wait! Where are you going?"

"I'm forsaking immortality for something better. Something different," Sunflash said. "I knew you were coming, so I waited to tell you."

"Something better? What?"

"That thing I worked a thousand years to be rid of. I've worked almost twice as long getting it back, but I've finally succeeded. Now I have a chance to be something other than what I am. The chance to be mortal again."

"I don't understand," Springshadow said. "We change all the time. We're foxes!"

He shook his head, smiling a sad smile. "We change appearance. Changing what you are requires reentering the field of time. Even gods can't do it. Only mortals. That's what makes them greater than any god. This is the 'Great Secret of Immortality' that The Den and Burrow Guide to Immortality hinted at. I had Summerstorm's example before me. To pay my debt to him, you will now have mine. Make of it what you will."

Guan Shi Yin reached down and took Sunflash's hand like a mother reaching for her child. "Time to go."

"Wait!" Springshadow said. "How do I get out of here?"

"Simple — you don't belong here," Guan Shi Yin said. "So any direction you go is 'out'. We'll meet again, I think."

They vanished. After a moment Springshadow let out a sigh. "Selfish bastard." It wasn't really an insult. Sunflash was, after all, a fox.

For a very long time, Springshadow did not vanish. She took advantage of her human form to sit down on a rock without having to deal with her nine tails, and she thought. When she finally left that place, she summoned her golden cloud and returned, not to Heaven, but to the Middle Kingdom. Specifically, to the mountain home of Wildeye. She found two of his disciples tending a fire inside the cave some distance from the entrance, and at the sight of her both men threw themselves face down on the earth, to Springshadow's considerable amusement.

"Gentlemen, I'm not who you think I am."

"I should say not," said a familiar voice, now full of exasperation. "Honestly, you two. You call yourselves my disciples and can't tell a goddess from a fox? Get back to your duties."

Looking rather sheepish, the two got to their feet and went back to tending the fire. Just within its glow Springshadow could make out the odd form of Wildeye. He greeted Springshadow courteously.

"To what do I owe the honor of this visit?" he asked.

Springshadow bowed. "I am in distress and have need of your counsel, Immortal One."

He raised one bushy black eyebrow. "Interesting. Let's go out into the sun and talk about it."

They walked out of the shadow of the cave. The air was thin and cold so high up in the mountains, but the sun was pleasant on Springshadow's skin, and far below she could see birds flying. Even the scraggly mountain pines were showing the bright green new growth of spring.

"You do have a lovely view," Springshadow said, "but I know you didn't bring me out here to take the air."

"I didn't want those two fools to hear what we might say," Wildeye said, smiling. "And by the way, you know I'm paying you no compliment when I say how lovely you look."

"No," she sighed. "It's an accusation. I understand this. In my youth I used a form such as this one to bewitch unsuspecting mortal men and drain them of their yang energy, which is how I reached my thousandth year. Shall we now dwell on how you achieved your immortality?"

His smile didn't waver. "That's the problem with old friends — sooner or later there are no secrets between them. I achieved this state neither through Enlightenment nor strict Taoist principles. Rather, I seized a bizarre stroke of luck and stole a Peach of Immortality from the Garden of Heaven. I am immortal only because I cannot be otherwise. You know the story."

"And yet you draw disciples."

He bowed slightly. "That was an accusation, too. And it's true. I can't beat them off with a stick. I know — I've tried. So they do what I say and think they're learning wisdom. In a way, perhaps they are. In the same way, perhaps, that your former lovers did. A hard lesson."

"But wasn't it wrong? I mean, of both of us? What sort of damage have we done?" Springshadow wondered if she sounded as miserable as she felt. Apparently so, because Wildeye raised his eyebrow again.

"Does this shallow contrition have anything to do with your exposure to Heaven?"

"I don't know," she said, "I just didn't expect Heaven to be so, well, ordinary. When I first heard the babble of voices through the portals, I couldn't believe what I was hearing!"

"What sort of things?"

"Divine scholars worried about their examinations. Trials and disputes. Large feasts and celebrations and music. Lovers' quarrels! It's all more refined and grand than the mortal world, but otherwise it's exactly the sort of thing I've experienced here in the Middle Kingdom for the last thousand years!"

Wildeye blinked. "Well, what did you expect?"

"Something to make what I have done worth waiting a thousand years for," Springshadow said. "Something better." Almost in tears, she related her meeting with Sunflash.

Wildeye didn't say anything for several long moments. He finally shook his head. "Springshadow, for a creature who spent a large portion of her mortal existence as a seducer and destroyer of men, you're charmingly naïve. How can one manage a disorderly cosmos? One cannot, and therefore order is essential. Even I know that the mortal world with its kingdoms, scholarly examinations, and hierarchies is simply a paler, shabbier plane of existence than the Heavens. A descent, if you like. You say you want something better? Heaven is better. I've been there and I know. But the one thing it isn't is different. Sunflash may have fooled himself into thinking he was doing you a favor, but in reality he chose what he thought was best for him. With the typical self-centeredness of a fox, he thought that it might be what was best for you, too."

"What if he's right?"

"Then that would be a fortunate happenstance. It does not add to Sunflash's worth. He waited on you to pay his own debts, not to help you with your own, no matter what he said. You know that."

"I know. Guan Shi Yin herself said that he wanted something from me, even though she seemed to think it a noble purpose. From what little I learned of Sunflash, I would dispute that."

Wildeye smiled. "It is the nature of the Goddess of Mercy to look for the good in people. Sometimes I think she creates it herself if she cannot find it. I've encountered goddesses of justice and gods of storm and war and demons and monsters from the bowels of the earth, but Guan Shi Yin? She's the only one of the whole lot that I truly fear."

"You're a reprobate," Springshadow said frankly. "And, I happen to know, a drunk and a lecher and a thief. So why are you so wise?"

He laughed. "I've managed to array Heaven itself against me. You have a rather odd definition of wisdom, girl."

"It is my own," Springshadow said. "As must be my purpose, if I am to have one. Thank you, old friend. I have much to do."

She took her leave from Wildeye, and only then did she return to Heaven. Specifically, to the Master of the Hall of Records. "Sunflash either has been or is in the process of being reborn as a mortal. Where is he now?" she said.

He frowned. "Why do you want to know?"

"Because I have far more respect for the wisdom and judgment of a reprobate Taoist immortal than that of a Heavenly Fox. Because, while it may be true that debts may be only delayed, not forgiven, it is also true that there is more than one way to settle a debt."

"Is that all?"

Springshadow thought about the matter, and not for the first time. She knew the course she probably should take; the way had been shown to her. If Sunflash was right that she would eventually have to abdicate her immortality and reenter the field of time, then so be it. However, if atonement was necessary, then first she had to understand what she had done to atone for. Right now she only knew of one single thing that needed pardon.

"No, Honored Sir, that is not all. I also wish to know what hell the man once known as Zou Xiaofan has been banished to."

"Again, may I ask why? You have no further business with him."

"With respect, I believe I do. A goddess once asked me why my first instinct was to appear as something I'm not. A god once asked me what truly mattered to me. I don't know the answer to either question, and I think I should know before I decide what I must do next. I think Xiaofan can help me with this."

"Why should he do anything for you at all? He has no reason to love you."

"True, but I know he does."

"Impossible. You put him in hell! I've seen the record myself."

Springshadow shook her head. "No, I only killed him. Apparently he understood the difference before I did, and I called him an idiot. It would be hypocritical of me to apologize for what I did to him since I would do it again, but calling him an idiot for understanding what I did not? I believe I need to apologize for that. What happens afterwards is something I don't know."

The giant bureaucrat sighed. "This matter is beyond me. I don't know if the Goddess of Mercy would approve."

"If you truly want to know the answer to that, then do as I ask. If Guan Shi Yin has something to say, send her to me. She will know where to find me."

The Master sent for the scrolls without further argument. Later, as Springshadow approached the dark gates of the hell where Xiaofan was confined, she found Guan Shi Yin waiting for her.

Springshadow sighed deeply. "I assume the Master of the Hall of Records took me at my word. Fair enough, but don't try to stop me."

"What if I do?" the goddess asked mildly.

Springshadow looked grim. "I'll fight you. I don't want to, but I will do it."

Guan Shi Yin smiled. "I know you fear me, and that is wise, yet you would test me if I got between you and your goal? Springshadow, I must say you've surprised me. You've discovered something you actually care about. Other than yourself, I mean."

Springshadow trembled. "What is this thing?"

"An obligation: the sort that Sunflash and Hsien Se spoke of. A small one easily discharged, I'll grant you, but your acceptance of it means that your quest is no longer just about you; and at least in some small way, you understand this thing that Hsien Se always understood and Sunflash finally learned."

"I know, and I hate it!" Springshadow said. "But I can't make the feeling go away. I've tried."

The goddess stood aside. "Then your nature is not now what it used to be. You've changed, just a little, and you managed that change while outside the sway of time. I must say I'm impressed. Go talk to Xiaofan, if you wish."

"I don't suppose you would take me to him?"

"Not this time, Springshadow, but please take this with you."

The goddess held out a small porcelain bottle, stoppered with a cork.

"What's this?" Springshadow asked.

"One of my tokens. You may find it useful where you're going."

Guan Shi Yin vanished, and behind where she had stood the gates of hell opened wide, but Springshadow did not move.

"She's gone. Wildeye, You can come out now," Springshadow said.

A large boulder beside the path flashed white and then swirled as if it had suddenly turned into mist. In another moment Wildeye stood beside her on the path.

"How did you know?" he asked.

"I may be in human form, but my nose still works. Stones don't normally reek of wine. You, on the other hand..."

"Point taken." Wildeye didn't say anything else for a few moments. And then he was almost hesitant. "Do you...do you really think you can do it?"

"Do what? Find Xiaofan without the Goddess of Mercy's help?"

He grunted. "No. I mean care about something that isn't you. How have you managed? I've been trying for centuries!"

"Then unlike Xiaofan, you actually are an idiot. The point of finding Xiaofan is to stop caring. I'll figure out how to rid myself of this 'obligation' thing, and that will be the end of it."

"Just in case that isn't the end, would you do me a favor?"

"What is it?"

"Teach me what you failed to unlearn."

She let out a sigh. "And you would chain me with yet another obligation? Is there no end to them?"

Wildeye grunted. "Don't ask me. You're the one going back to hell to find out."

Springshadow smiled at him. "Aren't you coming along? You may as well do it openly, if that boulder trick is the best you can do."

He frowned. "That was a good trick...and of course I am. I just didn't think you'd ask me."

"In your own way you've shared this adventure almost from the start. I suppose you have the right to see how it turns out."

"Then let's be on our way...before Guan Shi Yin returns. As I said before, she frightens me."

The two friends approached the open gates of hell, and without even a hint of hesitation they stepped right through.

About the Author

I've been writing and publishing fantasy and science fiction longer than I care to remember...or probably can remember. I'm originally from Mississippi and now live and write in the Mohawk Valley of central New York with my wife and a pair of grumpy cats. This book was a finalist for the Mythopoeic Award for Adult (as in grownup) Literature. I blog at "Den of Ego and Iniquity Annex #3", also known as:

WWW.Richard-Parks.com

Stop by anytime.

Printed in Great Britain
by Amazon